A World
of Difference

D1173419

BY HEATHER MCHUGH

Dangers
A World of Difference

A World
of Difference

POEMS BY

Heather McHugh

HOUGHTON MIFFLIN COMPANY

BOSTON 1981

Copyright © 1981 by Heather McHugh

All rights reserved. No part of this work may be reproduced
or transmitted in any form by any means, electronic or
mechanical, including photocopying and recording, or by
any information storage or retrieval system, without
permission in writing from the publisher.

Library of Congress Cataloging in Publication Data
McHugh, Heather, date
  A world of difference.
  I. Title.
PS3563.A311614W6   811'.54   80–23142
ISBN 0–395–30231–5
ISBN 0–395–30232–3 (pbk.)

Printed in the United States of America

P 10 9 8 7 6 5 4 3 2 1

Magazines in which the following poems previously ap-
peared are: *American Poetry Review*: "Hag," "High Jinx."
Aspen Leaves: "Breath," "Goods," "The Fence,"
"Whoosh." *Cornell Review*: "Kindling." *Green House*: "At
a Loss" (under the title "Pro Quo"). *Hudson River Re-
view*: "When the Future Is Black." *Madog*: "Elemental"
(under the title "Ten Acres"). *Moons and Lion Tailes*:
"The Nymph to Narcissus," "Brightness." *MSS*: "The
Meaning of Fall," "The Field." *The New Yorker*: "Retired
Schoolteacher," "Anniversary Song," "Toward an Under-
standing" (under the title "On Time"). *Paris Review*:
"Intensive Care," "North Island Songs," "Inside." *Plough-
shares*: "Message at Sunset for Bishop Berkeley." *Poetry*:
"Lines," "What the Old Women See," "Remains to Be
Seen," "Mind," "Elevated." *Poetry Miscellany*: "The
House," "Wrong." *Seattle Review*: "New Glasses." *Vir-
ginia Quarterly Review*: "Impressionist," "Damage."

"Toward an Understanding" (under the title "On Time")
was reprinted as the subject of a critical colloquium in
Carleton Miscellany. "Breath" was reprinted in *The Push-
cart Prize Anthology*. "Retired Schoolteacher" was
reprinted in *Poet's Choice* (*Tendril Magazine*). A group of
these poems was recorded for the tape *Blue Streak* pro-
duced by Watershed Tapes.

FOR KAREN TEPFER

Acknowledgments

Some of this work was completed with the help of a grant from the CAPS (Creative Artists Public Service) program of New York State. To SUNY Binghamton, for regular leaves of absence in which to write, I am very grateful.

There are a few people, in particular, to whom I want to express my loving gratitude. I got from my mother and her sisters a strong will and sense of independence; from my father, a passion for work. I owe my living to them.

And during the time when these poems were being written, it was to the love and companionship of two people, Gregory Biss and Jerry Mirskin, I owed my happiness. This book is also, especially, for them.

Contents

PART III

Part I

The Field

It was my day to study
in the field. I found
fences strung with glass beads,
small possessions of shock,
the farms of his and hers.
I couldn't make myself at home.
I lowed so the cow would
but the cow looked up, misquoted.
When I got back to the house
my five hired fellow-specialists
were taping their abstracts
to the window. Soon it would be dark.

The House

In evening purples, the kings
draw farther and farther away,

as absolute and cool as stars.
Dark brings its sexual power to bear

until the trees outside are huge.
Help, I tell the deaf man. Look, I signal

to the man with broken eyes. The moon
is in its seventh month; a truck goes by

with singing in its wake, an outside
chance. I've got to leave this house

where my uncle who has lost his hands,
my father who has lost his tongue

decide that everything is relative.
They cannot mean the world to me,

turning to themselves,
taking the window for bad art.

Like

Always I have to resist
the language I have
to love. This is my work,

as the girl reflected
in the cowpond studies
frequencies of throb.

The meaning isn't deep.
I don't say yes to please.
Polite, the politicians

drop their hat of names
but I forget the first
and family of them, for life

will not be memorized. Always
the days start longing for summer,
always the animals fall in love

but always like never before.

The Meaning of Fall

Gold leaf fell to the rake
and the fire. Leaping headlong
into those upholstered yards
we couldn't tell

rags from riches,
loving a little trash by nature,
having an orange crush.
But goods are made

by loss, and love becomes
a set of pet names, all
diminutive, and as for God,
we saw it was the dark

that made the stars. As time
went by, the jeweled movement
of the loan shark's car
would utterly impoverish the sky.

Blue Streak

During the twentieth century chance
was the form we adored — you had to
generate it by machine. Kisses came

in twisted foil, we quickened the clock
with digitalis, invented the pacemaker
in case we fell in love. The whiz kids

were our only ancestors; the buzz saw,
working west, had left its mark.
My children, this is history:

we made it; millions counted;
one-of-a-kind was a lie; and the poets,
who should have spoken for us, were busy

panning landscapes, gunning
their electrics, going
I I I I I.

Goods

I put my finger on it.
The value of silver
is not abstract; I love
how hot it gets.

Forget the model
of the girl, in favor
of her odd and only
clavicle, knuckles, lower back.

The man I thought was lost
is standing fast,
his longings in a briefcase,
and the past

is actual. I want to be held
to my word — no ghosted will and no
killed time. I love the wire to come
alive, the fork to be stuck in a fire.

Intensive Care

As if intensity were a virtue we say
good and. Good and mad. Good and dead.
What plural means is everything
that multiplying greatens, as if two
were more like ninety-nine than one,
or one were more like zero than
like anything. As if you loved me,
you will leave me.

*

You made road maps to the ovaries
upon your dinner napkin.
I forgot where I was,
in a state, in a sentence.
Absently stirring my alphabet soup
I had a mind to stay
with childhood's clean white calendar
and blueprint of the heart.

*

As if friends were to be saved
we are friends. As if beds
were to be made, not born in,
as if love were just
heredity, we know the worst; we fear
the known. Today we were bad
and together; tonight
we'll be good and alone.

9

At a Loss

Five quid for the sloth,
constructed of wickedness.
This is a value, says the auctioneer.
Ten for a fence to sit on.
How much for the sister of charity there,
or the synaesthesiac in the purple shirt?

A child in the crowd keeps asking who it is
that makes the icebox light go on.
In some back room a counterfeiter
mans his press. He's making money
toward his own pet senator and pair
of reproducing angels.

Now the wisdom tree is sold
as firewood, felled
by lightning, overharvesting, or just
an ax. The stroke could have cost us
our lives. Where

is the *genius loci* here?
The father tells the child there is
a little man in each refrigerator,
making light of cold.

Meaning Business

Gizmos and jeremiads aside, God
romped in a fit of glee, apropos
of nothing. He had no bailiwick,
no friends in higher places;
he hadn't an inkling, a sou.

The writers, meaning business,
came calling him names.
They wanted him to say the word
was the end, they wanted to live
for good. But God was a fool

for his own new feet, and a few
odd monosyllables of song. As long
as he lived, they'd have to
be content. Later, they could read
themselves into his will.

Confessional Poet

Busted and booked, and all
for love. We used to rip off
clothes and lie, steal time alone.
I was taken with him.

Let me tell you it's embarrassing
here in the haircut's architecture,
here in the secret chair.
I dwell on two antiques:
the moon, and the man that's in it
for me. We used to love the moving

amplitudes of radio, the earplug,
road map, facts faced like a blue clock.
Soon we'll have the afterlife
to love. And in the meantime

artists take to the networks,
cackling doppelgängers as their stunt men.
All you have to do is wive
your intimations, bring the house down.
Trash is material, truck of hunches,
fridges and ovens of dump.

After the frontal lobotomy
you know no one from two
in the echo chamber,
no one from Adam.

Conception

The big idea is light.
There on the tip of a pin
maybe seven devils see-sawed.
Soon from its cell the baby

was born to forget and be fat.
Have some peas, his parents said,
and use possessive pronouns.
So he did. He grew until

he managed to make
money and love alike.
His parents learned to die
but still he had to learn himself.

In the funeral crowd stood
children of his own, having hired
the vehicle and tenor,
having brought a certain

avoirdupois to the grave.

Dead of Night

The cat crackles, a rug turns
red, the doorknobs look alarmed.
These are surface charges.

Then the steps to the garden are gone,
leaves torn from their given names;
the dresses of stone women

are worn out — underneath is still
more stone. How much can the world
take of this nature? Deep in his sleep

the bombardier's afraid
the gardener is dead and all
the most expensive roses are about to fall.

Impressionist

1

I wasn't getting anywhere.
What good was the book
of matches, watch
of wheels, defective
mechanisms of my sex?
Where was the most of myself
I meant to make? Mistress
of the minded Q, the pointed I
I knew discretion comes to order
and the million likenesses add up
to one distinction, cells
of color on a riverbank

where the French
girl in the light
blue dress remembers
someone gone.

2

My mechanic lights a cigarette.
I'm at his desk, revising
the bill. I take a zero out,
I move a dot: this makes all

the difference. He wants
to sell me speed; I need it
like a hole in the head; my head
is overweight. I mean the world

to him. He'll fix my Comet,
I will feed his Milky Way machine,
I mean it matters, mud or moon,
what grounds we have for understanding.

Now I'm getting somewhere,
driving it home. The roadside leaves
are orange, yellow, every kind
of down. A dust of light

is in the drawing room, a dust of flowers
in the living room and in the bedroom, dust
has almost filled
the eyecup of the dead impressionist.

Message at Sunset for
Bishop Berkeley

How could nothing turn so gold?
You say my eyelid shuts the sky;
in solid dark I see stars
as perforations, loneliness
as blues, what isn't
as a heavy weight, what is
as nothing if it's not ephemeral.

But still the winter world
could turn your corneas to ice.
Let sense be made. The summer sun
will drive its splinters straight
into your brain. Let sense be made.
I'm saying vision isn't insight,
buried at last in the first
person's eye. You

should see it: the sky
is really something.

Part II

Brightness

Before history,
before you counted,
March was a day that went
lazing through slow
grades of gold.

The schoolyard wall
stood out so sharp
in some lights it could cut;
the sky kept cool
reserves of tincture and gauze.

A day was all you had.
You thought it huge.
And those forsythia —
so many whips about
to snap out yellow sound you felt

no one could sum them up.

Meantime

In the days when everyone said
oh boy and gee, when women
were stoled and muffed
and men would be men,
the hurricane her seventh birthday

was her first idea of sex —
that undomesticated power no one
could withstand, whose outskirts
bedraggled the trees. She suffered
an infatuation. Many ladies later,

she'd recall the proper name for this,
but in the meantime, something
had to be made of boys, who kept
cropping up. Windmill of ankles
and wrists, she had to turn

thirteen.

The Fence

Suddening one day by myself
I took my girlhood off and came
to understand the slugfests
of the forked and haloed boys.

I fell in love, by accident
and by design: its physics
was mishap. Every feather
of our burning wings was fixed

in Fibonacci series; every bush
was script with lash and spine.
It all made sense! My animals
danced, my spirits were artless,

I ran between them,
drumming the uprights
of the fence.

Wrong

I was the only amateur
in this academy of hate,
where others huddled
far from windows to recite
the proper names by heart
because they thought the heart
was memory. My memory was black

and I was no one's love
or luck, was no one's right
respondent, no one's pet.
I wrote and wrote, and I was always wrong,
under the long gas tube of light
you couldn't call
candescent, or available.

2

Around me moralists
disguised as social scientists
were saying shame and should and hush.
The noise was very white.
The students of descent were looking up
the words for tree, where money grew.
I'd come from the garden,
my name was mud and no one
knew my likes. I had to learn
the lesson of the gloves
before they held my hands.

And Still

Driving through woods in the goldenest
season, through shades and stripes
of filtered light, you enter
memory, the gardens of trembling
moment, moment of permanent
loss. You know you forget
and still you go.

Mind

A man looks at his watch to see
if he's hungry. Yes, it's eight,
he can imagine the whitefish,
white pepper, crème de la crème,
what his wife has made.
He says, You shouldn't have.
She says, Don't mention it.
The son grows thin.

At dinner the child tells a story,
what he saw outside: red hair,
a burning tree, a word on a sidewalk.
Mind your language, someone says.
He bites his tongue. At school

his days are numbered. He makes a felt
calendar, but that's not really the idea.
He has a hard time understanding
color is the frequency and not the object.
They keep asking, Now do you see?

Soon he'll be old enough
to take Criticism, practice saying
So-and-so sounds deaf, So-and-so
looks blind. Outside, the firetrucks
leave the scene, a safe grey street.

Whoosh

What summer hasn't shaken
its share of the flourishing
girls from arbors where, aloof,
they could forbear?

What summer hasn't brandished
swatches of daffodil *accompli?*
It makes a memorable decor, that
twisted Mississippi, with its five

willows for whoosh. The girl
you courted, pendant
from a swing, is there forever
in her weightlessness of veils

while the woman you married
once and for all walks out
in fall, in tight black pants,
and bears her heavy heart into the avenue.

Stall

Through memory and actual
mud, the woman approaches
the deep red barn
where animals stand
for anything — for years
of food, for good.

The woman is looking forward
to the day when everything is clear.
She thinks she's due for sunlight,
free from kin, but then

a moan from a downwind stall
reminds her of the man who had
his way with the dark in her.

Elevated

Fifty years the butcher shop
has hung these animals on hooks
to cure. The stationery store
dispenses the same old news,
same change, a little less silver;
ladies in a beauty shop desire
the perfect permanent.
Mornings this bright
cast the deepest shade;
everything seems to come
from memory. Even the subway's elevated.

Down the block toward the river Bronx
each yard has a chain-link fence, a dog
attracted to the random noise.
The woman no one knows is dead is still
in the chair by the bedroom plant.
Stripes advance from the blind
to her lap, slower than the human
eye can see. Above the accidents
of traffic you can hear
her clock and clean refrigerator hum.

Toward an Understanding

1 *On High*

Up here I love light, travel
light. Sun runs its slick
liquids down each arm
and wrist and fingerlake
on earth. Pack rat of scrap shine,
I catch the filaments of foil
that twist through green-brown tweed,
the bits of tin, the scattered
glass, pin money, sheet metal
(scissored and shivery) of lakes,
precisely wild.

Domesticated men, who do not burn,
but inch and pound out lives,
yell to low heaven!
I am above it all.

2 *On Insight*

Wool over eyes, soft
over shine, the clouds
begin to take the edge off
thought, the froth appearing
walkable and near, its grey
a density admitting no exception.
Now the ship of specialists begins
to sink, and my high hopes go under —
feet lap heart neck head in the clouds,
in the blind white folded deep.

3 *On Time*

We come through the ceiling
on dimmer wings. Streets widen,
paved with rain; the brown
pull's inescapable, we touch
down, I give up. I belong

in a house, in your arms,
in my own right mind. You'll fill me
with children, make me grave. I say yes,
let's get down to it, let
the darker things be saved.

When the Future Is Black

Maybe it's our nature to be naming
the degrees of color, times of heat.
I love you, and we're up in arms,

a shotgun wedding
where the present
is designed to keep

the past and future from forever
meeting. So the woman, calling
herself alone, expects to die like that;

and the man, who calls himself together,
goes from one state of affairs to the next,
thinking them discrete

like colors or decades made
to wheel, like destinations
made to map. Alive or dead, we make

a world of difference. Or so we say
as, over our heads, the sky turns
blue to red in a space of minutes.

Part III

What the Old Women See

The baby with his heavy head keeps tipping over.
On the sunlit porch his mother raises him up
and sings him songs of black and white.
The bleached sheets blow on the line.

In the shade of an alleyway four boys
are fighting, three on one. The one boy
won't give up. A woman and a man go by;
she's dressed in mourning; he is deep in thought.

Above the old men in the park
slow skeins of smoke arise, as though
a winter of woolgathering had to come undone.
They play their cards, swapping

what they know of the news, forgetting
the wives in their dark apartments.

Remains to Be Seen

We dress the boy in an orange cap
and show him how the gun is held.
He looks at his hand.

He likes five women, one in black
and one in yellow, whitey,
pinky and the naked one.

In all his stories he loses his heart.
We do not tell him that the truth
is just the future, that he's born

to die, and the love of the lovely
can kill. But we believe it.
He is beautiful, and at the movies

he is what we watch. His eyes
are fixed, his hair is smoking,
his whole face is blue.

Kindling

It is the age
of birth control and no
if I don't want.
You would father
tonight, this minute,
if I did. Instead

you nurse a cave
of hurts, you keep
the fireplace going,
lights off, eyes
black and burn.
I am right. You
are left. Between us,
the hearth and its rehearsals.

When my eyes have deepened
into far too cool a blue,
you quicken the coals with blowing,
make the nook grow brazen, cradle forth
the whistles and the rising
reds of pitch, till yes
it whispers, please
it whispers, feverish for sticks.

Damage

Evergreens are churning
black as wind. The trouble
goes deep, the doctor has a drill
of light for your eye. You burn
in the dark and you weep splinters.

Eye of the storm, you cannot fill
this hole. It wants the world,
a negative of a satellite or likeness
in a lake. You moon. You pine.
You don't see why.

Always far away, someone
who could have loved you
is awake, casually watching
night begin to fall
or day begin to break.

Language Lesson, 1976

When Americans say a man
takes liberties, they mean
he's gone too far. In Philadelphia

today a kid on a leash ordered
bicentennial burger,
hold the relish. Hold

is forget, in American.
On the courts of Philadelphia
the rich prepare

to serve, to fault.
The language is a game in which
love means nothing, doubletalk

means lie. I'm saying doubletalk
with me. I'm saying go so far
the customs are untold,

make nothing without words
and let me be
the one you never hold.

Hag

"a kind of light said to appear at night
on horses' manes and men's hair"
—Oxford English Dictionary

Horse gets into me, its mane
electric and its hooves

drumming up business. Men
get into me, having the hair

to go outdoors. I call
for order, but the cop's a cut

below; my songs
grow fur and hide.

Horse shoots up the spine, the arms
of stars, stopping what moves

in its tracks, stilling
what stones, owning

what stalls. Combed for romance, the moon
will always strand its caretakers. The groom

stands up in bed, ready to bridle
at a moment's notice. At night,

the fences down, the animals steal
from a newlywed's side, to wander

where a woman cannot come, who kept
her word but gave away her light.

High Jinx

Either they treed me or I hid
in the weed, or wash
was my overcoat or drink
was my wish. Either they missed

my face in the tea, or my stink
in the hash, or my hand
in the honeysuckle. I've been wanted
seven years and wasted more, been

burned, interred. Either they didn't
fertilize me, or I turned
to a desert rat, either I jumped ship
or they dumped me, I was game

or they shot my pool
with lily-killer. Man. Either you
used up your stunt juice or
my antibody grew.

New Glasses

A beautiful woman brings you
fortune. That is why they call her
fetching. She alone
can be herself, however close
the others come. But yours

is the mirror rich in irony;
it will not pay. All you can make
of yourself is the second person,
someone once removed. They tell you
beauty talks, and you shut up.
Deadeye in your new glasses

you see the red they speak of.
Now you have your mother's hair,
how she looked as she lay in the box.

Elemental

I want to last one more winter,
live in this austerity and learn
the elements responsible
for weeping, burning,
burying and song.

I want to hear the hours
of vibration in a glass of ice,
see the blues in the five-sided fire.
You aim your gun at the trembling
hill, and want the world to break

from cover. I say only
raise your hand against the sun,
darken my hair instead. Enter
into love as bare necessity;
the blueberry will turn ten acres red.

North Island Songs

The water that made the island
murdered the men. You can't expect
these moons to last, these fallen
roses, rising gold. You can't believe
in pure decor or easy virtue.
People are dying for good.

*

He wants other women,
those who never leave
well enough alone.
He's well enough.

At a distance I gather
what is going on. The dark
that fills the deep is the song
they hear in hulls.

*

If I pine and croon I am no woman
in my hooked heart, if I stand for lying,
maybe I can take a shine
and still keep cool. In its own element

that tough old bird the gull
hauls across the last-chance bars
and flashy waterfront its evening
seine of wail.

*

The dance turns out to be
a woodfire, fellows from the factory and mill,
a cop in the doorway looking nowhere,
and a kid to stamp our hands. The band
is bored by the third song and the man I'd like
to love is drunk in the corner, so
I plunge out the storm door to the cars and there

the stars are out. Orion perfectly
speared by a pine tree. Moon exactly
sharpened to a shade of meaning,
I can think then
cold and clear, imagine
why the inland people call
some kinds of water kill.

Anniversary Song

The picture of wedded
bliss wouldn't be
this kitchen window
cruised by gulls.
In every light they look
alike. After seven
years you don't watch out.

The food's begun to fasten
to the oven wall. In heat,
in heat. I have a man
in mind, in fact
he's out of sight,
making the clam beds pay
our debts. I am at home

with the clockwork birds, the time
I kill, the stew I'm in.
He's come to matter,
as the island comes
to mind. The world
of doubles loves itself.

Inside

In the field is a house of wood.
A window of the house contains
the field. You can't see far

with a sun in the sky, with a living-room
lamp at night. Locality is all
you light, and you, as single as a bed.

But there's no end to dark. The bed
is in the clearing and the clearing
in the wind; the world is a world

among others. With the stroke of midnight,
blind, a lover comes to make
the stars inside your cell begin to split.

Form

We were wrong to think
form a frame, a still
shot of the late
beloved, or the pot thrown
around water. We wanted
to hold what we had.

But the clay contains
the breaking, and the man
is dead — the scrapbook
has him — and the form of life
is a motion. So from all this
sadness, the bed being touched,

the mirror being filled,
we learn what carrying on
is for. We move, we are moved.
It runs in the family.
For the life of us
we cannot stand to stay.

Syllables

The island doesn't sink.
It's not a ship or spirits.
Doesn't try to keep up.
Doesn't care.

This comforts the lonely man.
He thinks like them he's given up
the ghost of likeness, line
and clause. But all along

the shoals of mated shapes
the boats will always growl
and run aground. It's farther out
that his survival finds its form:

where small and fat and striped,
and never to be touched, they sing
their whole notes, heard or not,
their boy low lub bob bell.

Lines

Some are waiting, some can't wait.
The stores are full of necessities.

The sun dies down, the graveyard
grows, the subway is a wind
instrument with so many stops;
even the underground comes
to an end, and all those flights

of fancy birds settle for one
telephone wire, the one on which

just now, the man in utterly
unheard-of love has caught
the word goodbye. He puts
the receiver back in the cradle
and stands. Outside his window

an old man with a hearing aid walks
aimless, happy just to be alive.

Breath

What I want from God, feared to be
unlovable, is none of the body's
business, nasty lunches
of blood and host, and none

of the yes-man networks,
neural, capillary or electric.
No little histories recited
in the temple, in the neck and wrist.

I want the heavy air,
unhymned, uncyclical,
the deep kiss — absence's.
I want to be rid of men,

who seem friendly but die,
and rid of my studies
wired for sound. I want
the space in which all names

for worship sink away,
and earth recedes to silver
vanishing, the point
at which we can forget

our history of longing
and become
his great blue breath,
his ghost and only song.

The Nymph to Narcissus

"*Si non se noverit . . .*"
—Ovid

We invented one
another, the way water
and air are intimate,
the way reflection
is a lonely art.
If you're smart
you know better
ways to suffer,
know yourself
insufferable.
Is this true?
Is this true?

It was for beauty
that we did each other in.
You longed for no one,
I was reduced to doubletalk.
This is no way to live.

Of course I turned to
nothing but bones and a voice,
then nothing but voice.
Of course you couldn't stand
the sight, your ground. In love

the secret is the self, in death
the echo of the secret.

Retired Schoolteacher

Brilliant planets float in that black lake.
She is losing her vision.
Her pupils are old.
All night long she stays up
trying to remember
an animal from the past,
imaginary, made
to swim in sight, to burn in tears,
to turn the heavens and the seas around.

On the coast of her youth
light-years away, she loved
to let the waves come over her.
Sleep, sleep. It is much too late
for children. That sinks in.
Deep in the dream and far
from all attachments she feels

the first of the starfish touch.